Acting Edition

Reykjavík

by Steve Yockey

|| SAMUEL FRENCH ||

FOR PRODUCTION INQUIRIES

UNITED STATES AND CANADA
info@concordtheatricals.com
1-866-979-0447

UNITED KINGDOM AND EUROPE
licensing@concordtheatricals.co.uk
020-7054-7298

Each title is subject to availability from Concord Theatricals Corp., depending upon country of performance. Please be aware that *REYKJAVÍK* may not be licensed by Concord Theatricals Corp. in your territory. Professional and amateur producers should contact the nearest Concord Theatricals Corp. office or licensing partner to verify availability.

No one shall make any changes in this title(s) for the purpose of production. No part of this book may be reproduced, stored in a retrieval system, scanned, uploaded, or transmitted in any form, by any means, now known or yet to be invented, including mechanical, electronic, digital, photocopying, recording, videotaping, or otherwise, without the prior written permission of the publisher. No one shall share this title(s), or any part of this title(s), through any social media or file hosting websites.

For all inquiries regarding motion picture, television, online/digital and other media rights, please contact Concord Theatricals Corp.

MUSIC AND THIRD-PARTY MATERIALS USE NOTE

Licensees are solely responsible for obtaining formal written permission from copyright owners to use copyrighted music and/or other copyrighted third-party materials (e.g. artworks, logos) in the performance of this play and are strongly cautioned to do so. If no such permission is obtained by the licensee, then the licensee must use only original music and materials that the licensee owns and controls. Licensees are solely responsible and liable for clearances of all third-party copyrighted materials, including without limitation music, and shall indemnify the copyright owners of the play(s) and their licensing agent, Concord Theatricals Corp., against any costs, expenses, losses and liabilities arising from the use of such copyrighted third-party materials by licensees. For music, please contact the appropriate music licensing authority in your territory for the rights to any incidental music.

IMPORTANT BILLING AND CREDIT REQUIREMENTS

If you have obtained performance rights to this title, please refer to your licensing agreement for important billing and credit requirements.

REYKJAVÍK opened October 27, 2018, at Actor's Express (Freddie Ashley, Artistic Director) in Atlanta, GA, as a part of a National New Play Network Rolling World Premiere. The production was directed by Melissa Foulger, with set and projection design by Seamus M. Bourne, costumes by Abby Parker, lighting by Ben Rawson, sound by Dan Bauman, and props by Melisa A. Dubois. The Production Stage Manager was Jude Futral. The cast was as follows:

JAMES. . . . . Gil Eplan-Frankle

DEBBIE. . . . . Stephanie Friedman

GRIGOR. . . . . Ben Thorpe

MARTIN . . . . .Michael Vine

PETER . . . . .Joe Sykes

NAOMI . . . . .Eliana Marianes

Subsequent Rolling World Premiere productions of *REYKJAVÍK* were at Kitchen Dog Theatre in Dallas, TX, and Rorschach Theater in Washington, D.C.

REYKJAVÍK was developed with assistance from the Kennedy Center for the Performing Arts and the National New Play Network.

CHARACTERS

JAMES – A young man, pretty and carefree, but his laissez-faire attitude comes from having lost a lot in life.

> Also plays:
>> **HANK** – A zealous, possibly immortal sex worker.
>>
>> **EBON** – An optimistic and very romantic raven.

DEBBIE – A woman, probably psychic. Debbie is not her real name but she's pretty chill about the whole "identity" thing.

> Also plays:
>> **LYDIA** – A pretty chill hotel employee.
>>
>> **AMBIANCE SISTER** – A magic presence, half of a whole.
>>
>> **INGRID** – An upbeat, pretty chill international stalker.
>
> And:
>> **HULDUFÓLK (F)** – A "hidden person."

GRIGOR – A man, murderous, patient, quiet except when passionately invested in "torch song" karaoke, possibly an invention.

> Also plays:
>> **LEÓ** – A very professional hotel employee.
>>
>> **AARON** – Unable to express himself.

MARTIN – A man, solicitous and very focused. He baits the hook, in love with his "good friend" Grigor, possibly an invention.

> Also plays:
>> **ROSS** – A man, a quality planner and decision maker.
>>
>> **ROBERT** – A lonely customer too willing to believe.
>>
>> **MAN IN THE DOWN COAT** – A mouthy drunk.

PETER – A man, a stoner, open-minded and that's a good thing, the kind of guy who just lets things happen.

> Also plays:
>> **MIKE** – A man, Ross's boyfriend, a cocky tourist.
>>
>> **DAVEY** – Deeply frustrated with his relationship.
>>
>> **HULDUFÓLK (M)** – A hidden person.

NAOMI – A woman, James' sister, with a bright pink stripe in her thick braid, and a lot of regret. Still uneasy after dying young.

> Also plays:
>> **LIL** – A hotel employee, not into her current gig.
>>
>> **VALERIE** – Gun-shy about love, always on the move.
>>
>> **AMBIANCE SISTER** – A magic presence, half of a whole.

SETTING

Reykjavík, Iceland.

TIME

Winter.

AUTHOR'S NOTES

[ ] indicate overlapping dialogue.

Licensees should retain the doubling outlined in the Character Breakdown as the doubling is specific to the storytelling.

The entire play takes place in and around Reykjavík, Iceland. All of the locations are ephemeral places, transitory, the kind of places people pass through or stop to rest but do not stay for long.

When the "torrent of blood" arrives during "Incisor," think more gradual dump bucket as opposed to a rain effect. It should read as a moment of abrupt violence.

About the Space:

The performing space could be relatively bare, only what's necessary, or maybe it's an avalanche of various and sundry items. It's open to interpretation and exploration. The only must is a nondescript bed. No matter what, light and sound are going to do a lot of heavy lifting here. There is also signage. It can be practical or projected (onto a wall or other surface), and it displays the location of each scene. Those locations are indicated with the phrase ***SIGN READS*** at the top of each scene. Maybe it also includes scene titles.

The location projections/practicals are distinct from the running projected dialogue throughout "Jawbone."

A Note on Songs:

The song that the Ambiance Sisters hum in the "Bittersweet" scenes will ideally be a slowed down, harmonized version of something like Blondie's "Call Me" or Cyndi Lauper's "When You Were Mine."

A license to produce *Reykjavík* does not include a performance license for "Call Me" or "When You Were Mine." The publisher and author suggest that the licensee contact ASCAP or BMI to ascertain the music publisher and contact such music publisher to license or acquire permission for performance of the song. If a license or permission is unattainable for "Call Me" or "When You Were Mine," the licensee may not use the song in *Reykjavík* but should create an original composition in a similar style or use a similar song in the public domain. For further information, please see the Music and Third-Party Materials Use Note on page iii.

1.

Jawbone

(SIGN READS: "An after hours lounge.")

*(**JAMES** sits in a round booth with a table in front of him, or it's at least an approximation of a booth. The table is covered with empty glasses. **DEBBIE** leans next to him. She's in a short slip dress and has a pair of large gold headphones on. She's fully unconscious. On the other side of **JAMES**, two men sit in the booth. **MARTIN** and **GRIGOR**. Everyone looks like they were going out to score.)*

(It's an after hours spot. The music is very loud. Bass heavy. It's difficult to hear. All dialogue is projected somewhere onstage.)*

JAMES. Thanks for the drinks.

MARTIN. You're very welcome.

JAMES. What?

MARTIN. You're welcome!

JAMES. It's really cool of you to buy so many rounds. I mean, I don't even know how many. I am officially drunk.

MARTIN. That's okay.

---

* A license to produce *Reykjavík* does not include a performance license for any third-party or copyrighted recordings. Licensees should create their own.

JAMES. And I'm not very good at math anyway.

> (**JAMES** *and* **MARTIN** *laugh.* **GRIGOR** *just sips his drink.*)

MARTIN. Are you feeling good, James?

JAMES. What?

MARTIN. Your name is James, right?

JAMES. Yes. I'm James. Did you, did you say your name?

MARTIN. I'm Martin. This is my best friend, Grigor. He doesn't speak any English. He really doesn't know what's going on, so just ignore him. But he knows when something looks good. He knows that much.

> (**JAMES** *lifts his drink to* **GRIGOR**. *The* **MAN** *lifts his drink back.*)

See, you're already friends. We're all friends.

JAMES. You're slick, huh? Did you, did you say where you're from?

MARTIN. Around here.

JAMES. Did you say you're from around here?

MARTIN. No.

JAMES. It is so loud.

MARTIN. Are you feeling good tonight?

JAMES. Oh! Oh, this is Debbie. I'm calling her Debbie, I don't know if that's right. She passed out for a minute.

MARTIN. We were hoping you'd come back to our room.

JAMES. What?

MARTIN. Grigor and I saw you over here by yourself and we hoped you'd come back to our room.

JAMES. I'm not by myself. I'm with Debbie.

MARTIN. She's your girlfriend?

JAMES. Oh no, no. I just met her tonight, she kind of crashed into my booth. I just mean Debbie counts as a person so I'm not alone.

MARTIN. And are you feeling good?

JAMES. You know, I am. I was kinda down earlier, but it's a fun night.

MARTIN. Down?

JAMES. Sad.

MARTIN. Why sad?

JAMES. This whole trip is a kind of, I came to see the northern lights. I promised someone I'd see the northern lights and I finally saved up the money to come here, but I haven't been able to see them. I kind of fail at things.

MARTIN. It's the middle of winter.

JAMES. What?

MARTIN. It's the wrong time of year.

JAMES. Fuck, man, that's what everyone keeps saying. And tonight's my last night here. I have to go back.

MARTIN. I'm afraid you won't see them.

JAMES. Well, I'm not gonna just stay in a bar all night.

MARTIN. So you are feeling good?

JAMES. You already, didn't you ask me that? I'm pretty fucked up but I think you asked me that.

> (*Suddenly* **DEBBIE**'s *eyes shoot open and she leans forward. Her voice is amplified and has reverb as she screams out...*)

DEBBIE. There's blood!! There's blood falling from the sky!!!

(The MEN stare as she relaxes back into her seat. They all start laughing. She smiles at them. Her voice returns to normal.)

DEBBIE. That was so insane!

(And she starts laughing. She lowers the headphones from her ears so they hang around her neck.)

JAMES. Debbie, you're so crazy.

DEBBIE. Who's Debbie?

JAMES. You are.

DEBBIE. Am I?

(They laugh. She's basically barely conscious. MARTIN taps JAMES to get his attention again.)

MARTIN. I have another question.

JAMES. Surprise me.

MARTIN. Are you feeling good?

JAMES. You did not surprise me.

MARTIN. But are you feeling good?

JAMES. Martin, I am feeling so much better than I was earlier! Fuck the northern lights and their cosmic game of hide and seek. They can fuck off!

MARTIN. You want to feel even better?

JAMES. I didn't hear you.

MARTIN. I asked if you want to feel even better?

JAMES. Always.

(JAMES laughs. MARTIN smiles, but it seems predatory. He looks over at GRIGOR and then

slips under the table between **JAMES**' *legs.* **JAMES** *is startled at first as* **MARTIN** *undoes his pants. He looks at* **GRIGOR**...*)*

Your friend is a show off, right? Oh, you don't speak English. You don't even know what I'm, sorry. Sorry.

*(***GRIGOR*** *lifts his drink to* **JAMES** *again.* **JAMES** *lifts his glass back and is instantly distracted as* **MARTIN** *goes down on him. He looks down*...*)*

Someone's gonna see you. Someone's gonna...

*(***MARTIN*** *continues.* **JAMES** *tilts his head back and enjoys.)*

Okay. Okay.

DEBBIE. *(To* **GRIGOR**.*)* Hey, you! Where did your friend go?

*(***GRIGOR*** *just stares.)*

Oh! Is he magic?

*(***DEBBIE*** *looks under the table and immediately sits back up, laughing again.)*

That's not magic! Am I magic? Maybe I'm magic. Oh, James. James!

*(***JAMES*** *looks over at her, still clearly enjoying himself.)*

JAMES. Uh huh?

DEBBIE. I just remembered I'm magic.

JAMES. Good.

DEBBIE. Let me read your palm. Give me your palm; I'm going to read it.

(She takes his hand.)

JAMES. You're reading my future?

DEBBIE. I don't know, let me look.

JAMES. Can you even do that?

(She looks.)

DEBBIE. Maybe. Maybe I'm an unconventional heroine. Maybe I see all the answers and then…

JAMES. Oh my god that feels good.

DEBBIE. Oh. Oh no. That's…that's awful.

JAMES. What did you say?

*(**DEBBIE** releases his hand and takes off her gold headphones.)*

DEBBIE. Nothing. I'm gonna get more drinks. But I want you to listen to this. You need to listen to this, okay?

JAMES. I'm kinda busy.

DEBBIE. You're not busy. He's busy.

JAMES. Okay.

DEBBIE. I'm gonna just…

*(She puts the gold headphones on **JAMES** and sets her MP3 player next to him. Just as she walks off, she presses play. **JAMES** inhales sharply and…)*

*(The club music suddenly dims to a dull thud, as if most of it is being cancelled out. The lights suddenly zero in on **JAMES**, a pin spot on his face and chest. A string quartet softly plays.* * *It's barely audible; as if it's coming from the gold headphones and we can*

---

* A license to produce *Reykjavík* does not include a performance license for any third-party or copyrighted recordings. Licensees should create their own.

barely hear it over the muted bass of the club.
GRIGOR *is still somewhat visible.* **MARTIN**
*is still moving under the table. But the focus
isolates* **JAMES**. *His eyes aren't any clearer,
but the world around him is stark. The words
just pour out of him in a waterfall and this
dialogue is not projected...)*

JAMES. My older sister Naomi used to show me pictures
of the northern lights in this big, coffee table book of
nature's wonders even though I was little and she was
already in high school and the photos were so gorgeous
and colorful, they were mesmerizing, and Naomi used
to promise me we would go there and she made me
promise her we would go somewhere really far north
and see those lights in the sky and I did promise, not
because I felt like I had to or anything, I wanted to see
them dancing in the sky, it was more than just the fact
I worshipped her, and I did worship her because she
let me feel like a part of things and she held my hand
in public because I was nervous around crowds and let
me pick the color for the pink stripe in her hair, she
had this amazing thick braid with a hot pink stripe and
it was wonderful and I never told my parents about
Naomi's boyfriends or how she would describe to me
what it was like to kiss them and I didn't know why
yet but it was magical and I never told them that she
would sneak out of the sliding door in her room that
led to the back patio and then knock on the window
so I could sneak into her room and let her back in
because it was just for us, no one else needed to know
and I didn't understand one morning when my parents
found that sliding door wide open, Naomi's room was
so cold and Naomi was gone, but none of her shoes
were missing and fresh snow covered any tracks but
why would she go barefoot into the snow, and I was
angry that she went to see the northern lights without
me until the spring came and the snow melted and they
found Naomi's jawbone by the creek, only her jawbone

and some teeth and nothing else, but it was enough to know she was never coming back and my life stopped and never started again and now I fail at everything, love, work, finding fucking lights in the...

(**JAMES** *yanks the headphones off and slams them down on the table. The music immediately blasts back up to the loud volume and the lights return to normal.*)

(**JAMES**, *breathing heavy, drinks his entire drink all at once. And he drinks whatever's left in another nearby glass.*)

You're, uh, you're doing a great job down there. What was your name again? Martin. Your name's Martin.

(*Pause.* **JAMES** *calms down and gets into* **MARTIN***'s rhythm. His eyes are closed.*)

(*After a moment,* **JAMES** *opens his eyes to find* **GRIGOR** *staring at him.*)

How's it going?

(**GRIGOR** *puts his drink down and smiles. He speaks at a regular volume, not trying to be heard.*)

GRIGOR. We put something in your drink.

JAMES. What?

GRIGOR. We're going to fuck you while you're unconscious.

JAMES. What? I can't... I can't hear you.

GRIGOR. Then we're going to kill you.

(**JAMES** *motions that he just can't hear anything.* **GRIGOR** *starts laughing.* **JAMES** *smiles at him, oblivious, and then makes*

*the familiar face of someone who is about to
cum...)*

JAMES. Whoa. Whoa, whoa.

(**JAMES** *pulls* **MARTIN** *up before he can finish
the job and uses his shirt to cover himself
while buttoning up his jeans.)*

MARTIN. Are you feeling good?

JAMES. Yes.

MARTIN. Come back to our room and you'll feel even better.

JAMES. I'm supposed to see the northern lights.

MARTIN. You will not be successful.

(Pause.)

JAMES. You're right.

MARTIN. But we will all be friends and feel amazing
together.

JAMES. I really... I want to feel amazing.

2.

Twelve Ravens

(SIGN READS: "A higher-end boutique hotel room.")

(A shower is running somewhere out of sight.)

*(**MIKE** enters from the bathroom. He's in a plush hotel robe and fresh from the shower. He's still using a comb on his damp hair.)*

MIKE. You really did a good job with this hotel, Ross.

(Pause. Then again, louder...)

You did a good job picking out this place.

ROSS. *(From offstage.)* Thanks! This is one hundred percent why I'm the only one allowed to book things when we travel from now on.

*(**MIKE** uses his hand as a flapping mouth to mock **ROSS**.)*

MIKE. Uh huh.

(He looks through an unseen window and something catches his attention.)

I'm glad we decided not to go out last night. Hey, those birds are still here. Those big, black birds are still in the tree outside the window.

ROSS. *(From offstage.)* What?

*(**MIKE** looks at the birds. The shower shuts off.)*

MIKE. Are you looking at me, birds? You all getting an eyefull? I feel like you probably have better things to do. Even though I am fun to look at, right? You know you like it, birds. I'm the handsome tourist of your dreams.

(**MIKE** *performs for the birds, a little sexy dance or something.* **ROSS** *enters from the bathroom. He's also in a robe, still using a towel to dry his hair. When he stops, he sees* **MIKE** *in front of the window.*)

ROSS. Are you showing off for the birds?

(**MIKE** *immediately stops.* **ROSS** *gives a big grin and kisses him.*)

MIKE. They like it.

ROSS. They probably think you have breadcrumbs.

MIKE. They were sitting there in the exact same position the whole time we were fucking. There are twelve. I counted. All in the [same places.]

ROSS. [Oh, Mike.]

MIKE. So they've already seen everything.

ROSS. It makes me feel really confident that you were counting birds in a tree while fucking me.

MIKE. I can totally do more than one thing at a time.

ROSS. Can you?

(**ROSS** *bends down and picks up a condom off the floor.*)

Come on. This is nowhere near the bed or the trashcan.

MIKE. I snapped it off and it, just give it to me.

(**MIKE** *grabs it out of his hand and disappears into the bathroom.*)

ROSS. Do you think we get to keep these robes? It feels like the kind of place where you get to keep them.

MIKE. *(From offstage.)* What?

(While **MIKE** *is gone,* **ROSS** *comes over to the window.* **MIKE** *returns and stands next to him.)*

ROSS. I think they're kind of creepy.

MIKE. It really does feel like they're looking at us, doesn't it?

(They lean in a bit. Maybe cock their heads. The birds are mesmerizing. Suddenly there's a knock at the door and it startles both **MEN**.*)*

ROSS. Jesus!

MIKE. Did you order room service or something?

*(***ROSS*** opens the door and a very formal looking concierge named* **LEÓ** *is there. He even has a little nametag. He has a card in his hand.)*

LEÓ. I'm sorry to bother you, gentlemen. Is all well with the room?

ROSS. Uh, yes. It's great.

LEÓ. Oh, how rude. I'm Leó from the concierge desk and I have a message for you from the ravens in the tree outside.

MIKE. I, uh... I don't understand.

LEÓ. Ah, it is rather unconventional, but the birds have an outstanding tenure here and we do our best to respect [their wishes.]

ROSS. [Wait, you have] a note from the birds?

LEÓ. They're quite bright and communicative.

MIKE. And you actually work here?

LEÓ. Yes, sir. At the concierge desk. As I mentioned.

MIKE. Okay. Okay, this is a joke, right? Some kind of Scandinavian joke?

LEÓ. Who would be amused by such a joke?

ROSS. Oh, do we get to keep these robes?

LEÓ. You are welcome to take the robes and a small fee will be expensed to your room.

ROSS. I see.

MIKE. Who cares about the robes?

LEÓ. Honestly gentlemen, I'm here out of respect for the birds and their long tradition of observing things at this hotel. If you'd prefer not to hear all that they now know about you, well, that is absolutely your prerogative.

MIKE. This is so bizarre.

ROSS. You're saying those birds, right there in the tree, know everything?

LEÓ. No, no, nothing like that. They don't know everything, it's not like the birds are gods or anything.

(He glances nervously at the birds.)

They can just see the things on this side of the hotel. Through the window. And some people believe them to be a bit... I'm not sure about the English word. Oracular?

MIKE. Oracular?

ROSS. You want us to believe these birds see the future?

LEÓ. Maybe I picked the wrong word.

*(Another knock and **LIL** enters. She is also from the concierge desk and is dressed accordingly with a little nametag.)*

Oh, Lil. Come in, please. This is Lil, she also works at the concierge desk.

*(**LIL** hands him another card and begins to leave.)*

MIKE. Is that another note from the birds?

> (**LIL** *turns around and mimes that she doesn't understand.*)

LEÓ. Don't do that, Lil. She's pretending not to speak English, but [she does.]

LIL. [Fine. Fine, I] speak English. I'm just really uncomfortable with this bird arrangement. It makes me uneasy.

ROSS. Why?

> (**LIL** *leans in, confidentially...*)

LIL. They know too much. When there were thirteen of them, it was less oppressive. But one of the birds, the most relaxed one, fell hopelessly in love with a guest and followed him away. Without that bird to keep the rest calm, the twelve left here are more "aggressive" [about things.]

LEÓ. [She's not saying] anything bad about the birds.

> (**LIL** *nervously glances at the birds.*)

LIL. I would, I would never say anything bad about the birds.

> (*Another knock and* **LYDIA** *enters. She is also from the concierge desk and is dressed accordingly with a little nametag.*)

LEÓ. Lydia, come in.

LIL. Hello, Lydia.

LYDIA. Hmm. Isn't this a little party?

LIL. No, it's not.

LYDIA. Oh, I see. Well, I have another card for you.

MIKE. Okay, and here's another "aggressive" bird note.

LYDIA. Hmm. Are they aggressive?

LIL. Yes, they are.

LYDIA. Perhaps it doesn't feel that way to me because I'm from here. But now that you mention it, they are quite worked up today, aren't they? I'm not saying anything bad about them, of course.

> (**LYDIA** *nervously glances at the birds then hands* **LEÓ** *the card.*)

LIL. Of course.

LEÓ. Of course not. Any more coming?

LYDIA. Hmm. It's hard to tell.

> (**LEÓ** *and* **LIL** *nod in solemn agreement. It is hard to tell.*)

MIKE. Is there anyone left at the concierge desk?

LEÓ, LIL & LYDIA. Apologies.

> (**LYDIA** *and* **LIL** *quickly exit.*)

ROSS. They're still staring at us.

LEÓ. This doesn't usually happen. You should be flattered. Or concerned.

MIKE. Concerned?

LEÓ. Probably flattered.

MIKE. And they have opinions? That they wrote down on little cards? Ostensibly with their little bird feet. Do we have booze in here somewhere? I want a drink.

LEÓ. I've never actually seen them write. However, yes, they are quite opinionated, but you didn't hear it from me.

> (*A raven caws from outside.* **LEÓ** *rolls his eyes.*)

LEÓ. They're also very sensitive. In any event, would you like the feedback?

> (**MIKE** *finishes pouring a drink and pulls* **ROSS** *aside.)*

MIKE. You're not buying this, right?

ROSS. Look, they have weird trolls for Christmas and think fairies live in the volcano. Maybe it's [just a custom?]

MIKE. [This wasn't in] any of those immersion books [I read.]

ROSS. [It'll be fun.]

MIKE. Or it'll be embarrassing.

ROSS. It'll make a good story.

> (**MIKE** *drinks his entire drink...)*

MIKE. Okay.

> (**LEÓ** *puts the cards into the order they were received and then hands them over.* **ROSS** *looks at one, then the next...)*

ROSS. Okay, well I can't read this.

LEÓ. Ah, of course. They're in Icelandic. I'll read them to you, how about that?

> (**ROSS** *hands the cards back.)*

Note one: "This feels like a new relationship, but it is clear to us from the intensity of their sexual congress that these men are well-suited to each other and will have many years of happiness together."

> (**LEÓ** *hands* **ROSS** *the card.)*

MIKE. Okay. That's...nice.

ROSS. Yeah, I like that.

LEÓ. Note two: "It is also clear to us that honesty would better serve these gentlemen and their potential future together as they are both clearly lying to each other during their sexual congress."

MIKE. What the fuck?

LEÓ. Oh, that one is more awkward. I apologize.

MIKE. We went from many years of happiness to just a "potential" future together [in one note.]

ROSS. [And what] does that mean, "lying"?

(**LEÓ** *hands* **ROSS** *the second card.*)

LEÓ. I'm not qualified to interpret for the birds. Would you like to hear the final note?

MIKE. Don't stop now.

LEÓ. Note three: "When the active partner…" Oh, goodness. I don't feel comfortable reading this one.

ROSS. Well we can't read Icelandic, Leó. So please go ahead.

MIKE. You don't want to piss off the birds, right?

LEÓ. Note three: "When the active partner removes the prophylactic without the knowledge of the passive partner, it does not bode well and could impact our initial judgment regarding longevity."

(**LEÓ** *hands* **ROSS** *the third card.* **ROSS** *awkwardly takes it.)*

If you need anything else, let us know. Enjoy your stay.

(**LEÓ** *quickly exits.)*

MIKE. So I mean…this whole thing is a bunch of bullshit, right? I mean, we shouldn't even worry about [these stupid…]

ROSS. [You said] the birds were watching you fuck me.

MIKE. That doesn't mean they know what they're talking about. They're, I mean, they're fucking birds.

ROSS. Did you take off the condom while we were having sex, did you?

MIKE. I mean, of course not.

> *(The birds go crazy with caws outside the window.)*

Oh, come on, shut up!

> *(The birds get even louder.)*

Fine! Yes! Yes, I took off the condom.

> *(The birds calm down.)*

ROSS. Have, okay, have you done it before?

MIKE. I don't know. Yes?

ROSS. Did it... Wow. I didn't think you would say "yes." Okay, I don't know, did it feel good? No, that's a stupid question.

MIKE. Look, it's not, like, in the grand scheme of things, it's not a big deal.

ROSS. It's kind of a big deal.

MIKE. I'm sorry. You know I don't like how the condom feels so [I thought...]

ROSS. [Got it, got it.] Just gimme a minute.

> *(And then something occurs to MIKE...)*

MIKE. Wait. So what were you lying about?

ROSS. Careful.

MIKE. You don't want to tell me?

ROSS. I don't know if I like all of this honesty.

MIKE. If I have to be honest then you have to be honest.

ROSS. Nobody's making you be honest.

> *(A quick burst of bird wings flapping and the lights in the room flicker. Briefly. Then it's clearly like they can't help or control this, they just become a flood of confessions...)*

MIKE. Sometimes I imagine what it would be like to tape [us having sex without telling you.]

ROSS. [Sometimes I can only get excited when] you're asleep next to me because I [know I could do anything to you.]

MIKE. [I have maybe an unhealthy obsession] with really built gogo boys and that's why I [never have any cash when we go out.]

ROSS. [When I go on business trips to Dallas, I] tell guys that I'm single and if [they try to touch me, I let them.]

MIKE. [Sometimes I get excited and] [forget that there's an "us."]

ROSS. [Sometimes I get excited] [and forget that there's an "us."]

MIKE. [I've been swapping pics with a guy who lives] about twenty minutes from us and he's young, [he looks maybe too young, but I like that.]

ROSS. [I get drinks with my ex, Johnny, every Thursday] after work and think about how things [could've been if I hadn't screwed that up.]

MIKE. [I never want to go to that Mediterranean] place because I got drunk and blew the bartender and I'm afraid you [could tell if you saw us together.]

ROSS. [I thought we were] [being monogamous.]

MIKE. [I thought we were] [being monogamous.]

ROSS. [When I'm on the train in the] morning, I position myself so my dick rubs up [against other guys' hands and if they respond then I...]

MIKE. [No, stop. Stop. I don't want to, I don't want to be saying] any of this!

> *(The lights briefly flicker again, breaking the spell. Pause.)*

What the fuck was that?

ROSS. You told me the bartender at the Mediterranean place was straight.

MIKE. Just because I blew him doesn't mean he's not straight.

ROSS. Double negative.

MIKE. And since when do you tell guys on business trips that you're single?

ROSS. Stop changing the subject.

MIKE. Fine, fine, I don't know what all that was, but the birds said we were lying to each other during sex. When they watched us just now, specifically. So that's all I want to ask about. We both lied, apparently a lot, but today, what was your lie?

ROSS. It will, it'll make it harder for you to...

MIKE. Yes? Harder for me to what?

ROSS. Just let it go. This was just some weird, unexpected thing and we can choose to forget [about it, right?]

MIKE. [No, do you] want me to ask the birds?

ROSS. Ugh, no, okay. I, uh... I know you take off the condom. I just never say anything about it because I know you like sneaking it off, like getting away with it. It makes it better for you to be taking advantage of me, for whatever reason, and also if I don't know about it then I don't have to take responsibility for it if anything… Oh wow.

(*Pause.*)

We are both liars.

MIKE. So then it's, I mean, everything's even.

ROSS. What?

MIKE. You've got your lies and I've got my lies, but like big picture…nothing's really changed? We're the same.

ROSS. Yeah. Except now we know.

(**MIKE** *and* **ROSS** *look out at the birds again.*)

MIKE. So maybe it's not as bad as it feels right now.

ROSS. The birds were right. We were well-suited for each other.

(*There's a single caw.*)

3.
Bittersweet (Part 1)

(SIGN READS: "A hidden room in the cellar of a nondescript building just off Hverfisgata.")

*(**HANK** is on a bed in long underwear. Barefoot. Reading a book.)*

*(Two **AMBIANCE SISTERS** in kitchen dresses, dirty aprons, and boots sit in chairs somehow outside of the space. Very "mom & pop butcher shop" in vibe. Maybe even aprons with dried blood. A large tin can filled with knives of all different shapes and sizes sits between them. They are also both reading books.)*

*(A bell rings three times in quick succession and then there is the sound of a lock opening. **HANK** puts down his book.)*

*(**ROBERT** enters. This is followed by the sound of a lock closing.)*

HANK. Nice to see you again, Robert.

ROBERT. Hello, Hank.

HANK. You're wet. Is it raining?

ROBERT. Just a bit of snow.

HANK. I haven't been outside. Snow? Really?

ROBERT. Yes.

HANK. That can work.

*(**HANK** snaps. The **AMBIANCE SISTERS** begin to hum a tune in beautiful harmony. It's like live background music and the room doesn't*

exactly get brighter, but somehow seems to warm. It comes to life.)

Of course there's snow. When you agreed to take me skiing, what did you expect? There has to be snow. We can't just sit by the fire the whole time.

ROBERT. Is that right? What if I want to sit by the fire the whole time?

*(**HANK** puts his hands on **ROBERT**, instantly intimate.)*

HANK. You promised we could actually do some skiing?

ROBERT. That depends on whether or not you're a good boy.

HANK. I'm a good boy.

ROBERT. Are you?

HANK. I'm such a good boy and you promised we could go skiing.

ROBERT. I did promise. But how can I take you out in public? I saw those other men in the lodge bar looking at you, Hank.

*(**HANK** takes a few steps back and coyly begins to unbutton his long underwear one button at a time.)*

HANK. But I can't help it if they look at me.

ROBERT. You were showing off. And you know how it makes me jealous.

HANK. I'm really sorry. I want to be good. I didn't mean to make them look at me like that.

ROBERT. You like it when they look at you.

HANK. No, I'm a good boy.

ROBERT. Admit you like it.

HANK. I only like it when you look at me.

ROBERT. Say I'm the only man you want.

HANK. You're the only man I want.

ROBERT. Be a good boy and say it like you mean it.

> *(He's almost finished unbuttoning his long underwear. He's very clearly wearing nothing underneath it.)*

HANK. You're the only man I want.

ROBERT. I don't believe you.

> *(**HANK** takes **ROBERT**'s hand and pulls him toward the bed.)*

HANK. I can show you.

> *(He starts kissing **ROBERT** and reaches inside his pants.)*

ROBERT. Wait, wait…

> *(**HANK** stops. The **AMBIANCE SISTERS** stop humming and the warmth disappears from the room.)*

I'd like to know your name this time.

HANK. It's Hank, silly. It didn't magically change. I'm not magic. Or am I?

ROBERT. What's your real name?

HANK. Oh, sure, Hank is short for Henry.

ROBERT. You know what I mean.

HANK. I don't.

ROBERT. What's your name when I'm not here?

HANK. That's such a bizarre question.

ROBERT. I want to know.

HANK. It's good to want things.

ROBERT. You're not going to tell me?

HANK. You're being so serious. And I don't remember ever admitting that my name isn't Hank. Is your real name Robert?

ROBERT. Yes.

HANK. Huh. You don't look like a Robert, if I'm being honest.

ROBERT. If you're being honest.

(**HANK** *gives a good-natured chuckle.*)

HANK. I'm sorry, I didn't realize you were paying for an honest sexual fantasy.

ROBERT. That's fair.

HANK. Clearly I want you to feel special, so don't [take this as...]

ROBERT. [You want me to] "feel" special?

HANK. You are special.

ROBERT. Huh.

HANK. If you don't like the skiing thing, the snow thing, I can make up something else. Maybe something less conventional? Just give me an idea of what you're in the mood for tonight.

ROBERT. Maybe tonight we can just talk?

HANK. Talk.

ROBERT. About you?

HANK. With all due respect, that's really boring. Come on, I'm going to figure out what you want; I'm good at it. So just save yourself some valuable time and tell me. Oh, we can do the ocean thing? The boat? You like that one.

ROBERT. I do love the, I really love the ocean thing. But I'm, no, I'm telling you I want to know about you: where you're from, how you ended up here, what your life is like when you're not working?

HANK. Why?

ROBERT. How many times have I been to see you?

HANK. Honestly, Robert, I've lost count.

ROBERT. Right? And I keep coming back because I'm so curious about you. Whoever you are when you're not... this.

HANK. Okay. I'm going to sidestep that implied judgment. That's okay.

ROBERT. I wasn't [trying to...]

HANK. [I said it's] okay. But I think the reason you keep coming back is because I'm a really good fuck and you have really specific fantasies.

ROBERT. So tonight I want to talk about you. That's my fantasy tonight.

(**HANK** *takes this in.*)

HANK. You want to know about me?

ROBERT. Yes.

(**HANK** *kneels on the bed. He slips out of the top of his long underwear and ties it around his waist. He sits down and snaps. The* **AMBIANCE SISTERS** *begin to hum a tune in beautiful harmony. The room somehow seems to warm. It comes to life again.*)

HANK. Go for it. Ask me anything.

(**ROBERT** *cautiously sits on the edge of the bed.*)

ROBERT. How old are you?

HANK. I don't know.

ROBERT. You don't know?

HANK. I came here when I was little and I don't exactly celebrate my birthday, so I don't know.

ROBERT. When you were little…you came here?

HANK. Yes.

ROBERT. Okay. That's…unusual.

HANK. Is it?

ROBERT. What do you do when you're not working?

HANK. I don't understand the question.

ROBERT. When you leave here at night, or in the morning, when you leave here where do you go?

HANK. I don't leave here.

ROBERT. What?

HANK. You see that window up there?

ROBERT. Yes.

HANK. When I was younger I used to climb up there and look out sometimes, even though we're not supposed to, and I'd watch the world. But at some point I stopped doing that and just accepted that this is my world.

ROBERT. You don't… You can't mean you never leave this room?

HANK. I go down the hall for a shower after each appointment. If I need one, but I don't always need one. But that man in all black who buzzed you inside, he's always with me.

ROBERT. Oh my god.

HANK. What?

ROBERT. You're telling me you're a prisoner here.

HANK. Don't think of it like that; they just take care of me.

ROBERT. Hank.

HANK. Stop looking at me like it's bad. It's not bad, is it?

ROBERT. This is worse than I ever, we have to, we have to get you out of here. Right now.

HANK. I can't leave, they won't let me.

ROBERT. I can, I can bring the police.

HANK. No, don't. Robert, you don't understand. Please, if I don't perform for you then they'll punish me. You have to tell them I did a good job. You can't tell them I told you any of this.

ROBERT. But I [have to...]

HANK. [Please, the] best way you can help me is to just let me perform for you.

> (**HANK** *leans forward and rests his hands in* **ROBERT***'s lap.*)

ROBERT. I don't, if you just...

> (*They kiss. Then* **HANK** *laughs proudly and sits back on the bed. He looks incredibly pleased of himself.*)

HANK. I told you I'd figure it out.

ROBERT. What?

> (*Suddenly the* **AMBIANCE SISTERS** *stop singing and the light shifts back.*)

HANK. You're hard right now.

ROBERT. Hank, what the fuck?

HANK. I felt it. You're hard. You've got a serious rescue complex and you want to be the big strong man that saves the young boy, right? I know I'm right. Okay, okay, I can work with that.

ROBERT. None of that was real?

HANK. Are you serious?

ROBERT. I told you I wanted real answers.

HANK. And I told you it's good to want things.

ROBERT. I can't believe you.

HANK. First of all, it's what you paid for and, second, you got excited so I think I kind of nailed it.

ROBERT. That was a fucked-up trick to [play on me.]

HANK. [It's actually] pretty common for gay men to have this protective thing for a younger guy. It's like they think they can spare them some of the pain that they went through, something [like that.]

ROBERT. [I wasn't] doing that.

HANK. And also, maybe they want to control something young and vital, at least that's a part of it. Like, a little bit of ownership. Oh, and of course, they want the sex. They think we don't know.

ROBERT. So we all just fit into these little fucking boxes for you?

> (**HANK** *snaps. The* **AMBIANCE SISTERS** *begin to hum a tune in beautiful harmony. The room comes to life again.)*

HANK. I'm not talking about you, Robert. You're special.

ROBERT. Fucking stop it.

> *(The music cuts out. The lights restore.)*

HANK. Why are you getting angry? I'm honestly not trying to make you angry. You want to see behind the curtain and I'm telling you that's not going to happen because I'm just a fantasy and there isn't anything behind it. It's like going to a strip club or getting, I don't know, a "private" massage. You know in the back of your head it's a transaction; you're just making me say it out loud. But if you're willing to forget it, I will too, and we can go back to indulging any amazing thing you want.

ROBERT. I just want to know who you are.

HANK. You. Tell. Me.

(**HANK** *smiles at* **ROBERT**. *Pause.*)

ROBERT. I'm going to leave.

HANK. Why?

ROBERT. This isn't what I want.

HANK. Look, you're just going to come back. All the men like you come back.

ROBERT. I don't think so.

HANK. Well since you have to make an appointment, I'll know you're coming.

ROBERT. I said I don't think so.

HANK. Robert, that's... I think that's a real shame.

ROBERT. All the time I've spent here. I really thought this was...

HANK. What?

ROBERT. Special.

HANK. I'm sorry you still don't understand. But listen if you really think you're not coming back, we should do the ocean thing. Or you should at least let me fuck you one last time.

4.

Tongues

(SIGN READS: "A very different, much less expensive hotel room.")

*(**EBON** and **PETER** are in bed. They've been there for a while. **PETER** is in briefs, maybe a T-shirt. **EBON** is naked. We might not be able to see it entirely, but he has small, dark wings tattooed on his back. The mood is intimate, playful, and they're seriously high. They're sharing a joint.)*

EBON. What is this?

PETER. It's a blend.

EBON. Oh.

(Pause.)

A blend of what?

PETER. Indica and Sativa.

EBON. Oh.

PETER. It's good, right?

EBON. My head feels funny.

PETER. Shhh. That means it's working.

EBON. Okay, good.

*(He snuggles closer to **PETER**.)*

PETER. It's so crazy that we connected like this. Isn't it crazy?

EBON. It's not that crazy. I was following you for a while.

*(**PETER** laughs it off.)*

PETER. Uh huh.

EBON. I was like, "That guy. That's the guy."

PETER. Yeah?

EBON. Yep.

PETER. I've never been, like, a "fate" kind of guy. God, that sounds way too… Anyway, I've never really thought about people that way, that they can kind of fit, I don't know, but there's something about you, Ebon.

EBON. I'm pretty great.

(*They both laugh. Still passing the joint.*)

PETER. I feel like I can be myself with you.

EBON. Who else would you be?

PETER. I mean, like, I can relax and, it's stupid. I'm being stupid.

EBON. No, no. I get it. I think?

(*He begins to exaggerate his words.*)

Peter gave me pot. Wow. I can feel the words in my mouth.

PETER. That means it's working more.

EBON. Oh, good.

PETER. Just I've spent so much of my life, I'm gonna get grand now. Not grand, I'm gonna tell, like, an origin story. That's…is that less grand?

EBON. It's still pretty grand.

PETER. Yeah. If you'd rather just be quiet together and zone out we can…

(**EBON** *kisses* **PETER.** *After a moment,* **PETER** *breaks away with a laugh.*)

You have a…

EBON. What?

PETER. You have an aggressive tongue.

EBON. Maybe you have a lazy tongue.

PETER. Huh.

EBON. Just tell me your story.

> (**PETER** *hops up on his knees and claps his hands, rubbing them together. He's getting ready to tell the story and it's adorable.*)

PETER. Okay. Okay, when I was little, not little, when I was about thirteen I guess? I used to always go to this bookstore near our house. A chain place, before bookstores vanished.

EBON. Bookstores vanished?

PETER. Yes? I don't know, I've never tried to tell this story before. Do you have bookstores here?

EBON. We have a lot of bookstores. People have an, uh, a healthy love of books.

PETER. Okay. Well, over in the U.S. most of the bookstores went away. Or they kind of went everywhere then went away. Like when you light a match.

> (*He mimes what happens when you light a match, it flares up, and then quickly goes out.*)

Anyway, I told my parents I was meeting other kids for this role-playing game. But I never actually played. I had this bag I took, but it was always empty, right? My mom would drop me off and I'd go inside, walk past the other kids, and set up camp near the magazine section. And when no one was looking, I would take one of the adult magazines. Like, I would take the ones with the naked guys, there were a few.

EBON. Because it's fun to look at naked men.

PETER. Yeah, but also...I'd actually take the magazines. I'd steal them, put them in my bag and take them home. I took a lot of them. But magazines only come once a month, ya know? And I needed more than that, more material. So over a couple weeks, I started drifting into the photography section. There were all of these books, like big art and photography books, with pictures of naked men.

EBON. And you looked at those, too.

PETER. And I took those, too. Because I'd look at them at home and ya know...

> *(He mimes jerking off.)*

But also, I kind of got off on taking them. The danger. It wasn't just about getting caught stealing. It was about getting caught being gay.

EBON. No one knew?

PETER. Are you crazy? No, no one knew. For a while...

> *(He takes a long drag off the joint and exhales
> a cloud of smoke.)*

But I had this collection, like this little library of books and magazines hidden in my closet. In my room. Like, a stack of magazines this tall and an even taller stack of these hardcover books.

> *(He illustrates the heights. He clearly stole a
> lot of material.)*

And it got to the point where I couldn't sleep at night because I was so terrified my parents would find them. And maybe I felt...guilty. So one day I just sort of, have you ever just decided something? Like, this is it, I'm going to complete this thing and I have to do it?

EBON. I know that feeling.

PETER. Right?

(**EBON** *seems almost reflective. But he might just be high.*)

EBON. Yes.

PETER. So one day I announce that I'm going to clean out my closet. And my mom is thrilled because she doesn't go in there, but she knows it's like a disastrous little pocket universe of junk.

So I put a bunch of stuff into one of those big black trash bags. And I carry it downstairs through the den, where my folks are watching, I don't know, probably a football game. And my mom looks up and says, "Wow, you're really doing it. I'm impressed." My dad kind of glances from behind his newspaper and doesn't say anything. I keep going out to the garage. And as I'm dropping this bag into the trash can I feel like a genius because this is working. So that was the test bag, right? Success.

Back in my room, I load up a second trash bag with all of the magazines, all of the books, any evidence that I'm a gay thief. And I head downstairs.

But this time my dad stops me. He says, "You're throwing away another bag of stuff?" And, totally eclipsed by fear, I say this is the last of it. My mom says it seems like a lot and she doesn't want me just throwing away things instead of cleaning. I start to stammer, my brain short-circuiting.

And in that crystal clear moment, my dad asks: "What exactly is in there?" I have no idea what my face looked like, but they both looked at me like I turned seven different colors. I kind of choked out: "Please just let me throw this away and I'll be done!"

My dad said, "You need to calm down. Leave that bag right there and when we're done watching this, we'll go through it and see what to keep. In fact, just dump it out right there..."

PETER. I should have run. I wanted to die. My heart was slamming in my chest and I thought, "This is it. This is when I break my mom's heart and my dad throws me away." But I just, I dumped out the bag onto the den floor. Everything came out in this collage of images of naked men, some high art, some immediately dirty, some explicit. It was clear these were things I shouldn't have, but I think it took them a minute to realize there were no pictures of women. And then they both looked up at me.

I was paralyzed and dizzy. And then... – this thing happened, this self-preservation thing, and I started crying and my tongue started dancing, all on its own. This story just spilled out: how all my friends started liking girls and I hadn't, so I took this stuff to see if I might like guys, but then I started liking girls so now I was getting rid of all of it because I didn't need it and I'm so stupid.

   (Pause.)

Then I watched my parents, two very intelligent people, decide to believe this lie rather than face the alternative. And I became two people, right in front of them. I learned how to do that. Almost automatically.

My dad made me put everything into a grocery bag, like one of those brown paper bags, and get in the car. Without speaking, he drove me to the bookstore and walked me inside. He asked for the manager and a man came out, round glasses and a ponytail. I recognized this man, from all the time I'd been spending in his store. And he recognized me. Without looking at me, my dad said, "My son has been taking things from your store. We'll handle it however you think best."

The manager was upset. But then he looked in the bag.

I could feel him looking down at me. So I looked up at him. And his face, I've still never seen anyone look so sad or sympathetic in my entire life. I was too young to know he didn't need to say anything, that he couldn't say he was like me, and he had probably been through too much in his own life to punish me. So he just sort of quietly said I should never come back in the store. And we left.

EBON. Light this again?

> (**PETER** *lights the joint again.* **EBON** *takes a drag.*)

What happened when you got home?

PETER. Nothing. We never talked about it again. I was an only child and they sort of had everything pinned on me so it was easier to believe it was just, like, a misunderstanding.

EBON. I can't imagine that sort of, I mean, I had twelve brothers so my parents barely knew my name.

PETER. Twelve?

EBON. Yes.

PETER. Wow.

EBON. That's...an intense story.

PETER. I think it's...whatever, it's hard to look at your own life like it has these key moments. But like I said, I think it's when I learned how to be two people. And then I never stopped being two people. Even after I came out.

EBON. I understand.

PETER. Yeah?

EBON. Yes.

PETER. That's what I mean, just even telling that story. I just feel so comfortable around you and it's only been a couple days. But it's like I don't need to be whatever those two things have become and I can just...be me.

EBON. It's because we're in love.

PETER. You're so sappy. You think we're in love?

EBON. Yep. That's why you told me the story you've never told before.

PETER. Huh. Maybe we are.

EBON. And probably because I'm two people, too.

PETER. Oh, yeah? How's that?

EBON. Well, actually I'm a person and a bird.

PETER. Like, spiritually.

EBON. No, I was very attracted to you, sort of intrinsically, so I turned into a person. But I'm a bird. A raven, actually. Like a really handsome one.

PETER. Okay. And you turned into a person?

(**EBON** *examines his own hands.*)

EBON. I didn't even know I could. How about that?

PETER. This is...this is the first time you've smoked pot, isn't it?

EBON. Yes.

PETER. Okay. So what happens if we fall out of love?

EBON. I don't know. I guess I turn back into a bird? Maybe go back to the tree where all my brothers live outside of this fancy hotel?

(*Pause.* **PETER** *starts laughing.* **EBON** *can't help but laugh with him.*)

What?

PETER. You're really high.

EBON. I am really, really high.

PETER. And I'm two people and you're two people.

EBON. Well, a person and a bird.

> (**PETER** *kisses* **EBON**. *They are all smiles as* **PETER** *gets out of the bed and heads into the bathroom. As he goes…)*

PETER. Don't turn into a bird.

EBON. I'll try really hard not to, okay?

> (**EBON** *leans back and takes another hit off the joint. He exhales and smoke fills the air around him.)*

But sometimes things just happen.

5.

Incisor

(SIGN READS: "In the street just outside of a bar on Klapparstígur.")

*(**AARON** tumbles out of a bar onto the sidewalk. **DAVEY** is a few seconds behind him. They are arguing. And drunk. It's clearly cold outside. Light from a neon sign in the bar spills onto the street, but the guys aren't really in it.)*

AARON. Stay if you want to stay, I'm going back to the hotel before dinner.

DAVEY. Aaron, I'm not gonna stay by myself.

AARON. Whale meat and beer isn't exactly my thing. And I feel like you won't be by yourself for long.

DAVEY. Fuck you for that and how is it already dark outside?

AARON. See you at the hotel.

DAVEY. Okay. This is about last night and I wish you'd just fucking say that out loud instead of whatever this, instead of this little performance.

AARON. Oh, Davey. You're. So. Wise.

DAVEY. But this dramatic exit is your [way of...]

AARON. [Dramatic?]

DAVEY. Here's a thought: come back inside and stop making things shitty.

AARON. I didn't bring some guy back to our room, so how am I [the one who...?]

DAVEY. [No, that's right.] I'm the one who did that.

(He announces to the entire block…)

I did that! I brought a guy back to the room last night. He was a drunk Scottish guy, if you're keeping score. I could barely understand him.

AARON. I'm sure meaningful conversation was very important.

DAVEY. Maybe I have questions about Scotland?

AARON. Circumcision, yes or no?

DAVEY. So, I've admitted to bringing a guy back, great, and what did you do about it? Nothing. You didn't do a damn thing [about it.]

AARON. [Fuck off.]

DAVEY. No, so what am I supposed to think? I come home [with this…]

AARON. [I can't fucking] [believe you.]

DAVEY. [I come home] with this hot guy, and you pretend to be [asleep, so…]

AARON. [The fact you] think that guy was hot shows how [drunk you were.]

DAVEY. [You're "asleep,"] so we go in the bathroom, probably to fuck around for a few minutes.

AARON. An hour.

DAVEY. Whatever.

AARON. A loud hour.

DAVEY. Well, he had stamina. And you didn't do shit about it. You just laid in bed and what? Suffered through the indignation?

AARON. Was it a test?

DAVEY. Because if you wanted to say something and instead just laid there silently [then that's pretty…]

AARON. [Was it a] fucking test?

DAVEY. Sure maybe.

AARON. Bullshit, you were fucked up and had a hard-on for some [guy you met…]

DAVEY. [I can be, I] can absolutely be fucked up and hard and still testing you.

AARON. It's funny how your whiskey dick doesn't come into play with strangers.

DAVEY. I can think of another [word for it.]

AARON. [So I failed] your test that wasn't a test and I wouldn't even know it was a test if I hadn't brought it up, so what's your point?

DAVEY. My point is most guys, most guys who are in love, would fucking say something if they felt disrespected or left out or whatever the fuck you felt. Not just lie there and listen and suppress their feelings into this passive aggressive bullshit I've been dealing with all day. You can be pissed off. You can fucking say something!

AARON. This is night two.

DAVEY. What?

AARON. This is night two of a five-night trip and you wanna open the Pandora's box of our relationship on a random sidewalk in front of everyone?

DAVEY. Who knew we had a "Pandora's box" of problems to open? And there's not even anyone around and why does it matter what day it is?

AARON. It's going to make the rest of the trip really awkward.

DAVEY. Wow.

AARON. Clearly you don't care about that or you'd calm the [fuck down.]

DAVEY. [Even when your] words say "I'm angry" you still crush it down. It's like some horrific parlor trick.

AARON. Me choosing not to make a fucking scene is horrific?

DAVEY. Listen. Listen to me, when I bring a guy back to our hotel room and suck his dick five feet away from you, and that's what those loud sounds coming from behind the door were, why don't you say anything?

AARON. Like what?

DAVEY. That it's not okay for me to treat you like that.

AARON. I know.

DAVEY. Then say it! Ya know, maybe I knew you were awake. Or maybe I just really hoped you were awake and that you'd actually fucking stand up for yourself. Or be jealous. Or show any kind of anything, I mean goddamn.

AARON. I was jealous, or fucking angry, and wanted to bash his head into the countertop, okay?

DAVEY. More words.

AARON. Well, I'm not actually going to bash some guy's head [into the counter–]

DAVEY. [Why not?]

AARON. Because that's insane, Davey. Look, fine, fine. Fine, I won't go back to the hotel. Can we just go to the restaurant? I made these reservations like a month ago and this place is [supposed to be…]

DAVEY. [The level of, like,] compartmentalizing in your brain is fucking stunning.

AARON. I just don't want to fight with you!

DAVEY. You were right; the next three days are going to suck because we are fucking done.

AARON. That isn't going to work for me so what else do you have?

DAVEY. Classic. Do you have any idea how terrifically fucked up it is that everything in our relationship, ours, has to work for you?

AARON. Clearly not everything.

DAVEY. Okay, you don't accept the breakup. Why?

AARON. Because I love you, okay?

DAVEY. In the abstract, yes, in the abstract that is the correct response, Aaron, but it's completely devoid of any [meaning or context.]

AARON. [Now you're just] punishing me.

DAVEY. No, no, I'm not. I'm coming to terms with the fact that you're all up in your head and sometimes your dick and nothing in between. It's intellectual, it's all what you think you should do or say and never what you want to do or say.

AARON. You don't know shit about what I want.

DAVEY. Whose fault is that?

AARON. Mine? Is that my grand revelation [in a foreign land?]

DAVEY. [Over a year we've] been dating, a year, and whenever you say you love me I think, "How could he possibly love me?" Because I do terrible things, I don't share my feelings with you in any meaningful way, you don't really know me. What's my favorite band?

AARON. Please. You're obsessed with Fleetwood Mac.

DAVEY. No, you're obsessed with Fleetwood Mac. My favorite band is Hole. What kind of dog have I always wanted us to get?

AARON. This is stupid.

DAVEY. A Basenji because they don't bark and act like cats.

AARON. Then why don't we just get a fucking cat?

DAVEY. You have some idea in your head of who I'm supposed to be and you ignore the rest and then have the balls to act disappointed all the time. I disappoint you so much that I actively find reasons to not see you. Did you know that? I feel like I'm hiding in my own life.

AARON. Like you're so perfect.

DAVEY. I just, I just said I'm not! I'm, in fact, I'm so far away from perfect. But if you think you're in love with me and you honestly haven't seen any of the things I'm talking about then you're delusional!

AARON. We're just, we are different people. We handle things differently.

> *(***DEBBIE*** *falls out of the bar into the neon lights near the* **MEN**. *She's in her same slip dress, but she left her gold headphones with* **JAMES**. *A* **MAN IN A DOWN COAT** *follows her.* **DEBBIE** *is laughing.)*

DEBBIE. I am not going home [with you.]

MAN IN THE DOWN COAT. [But I'm gonna] make you feel so good.

> *(***DEBBIE*** *grabs his palm and looks at it.)*

DEBBIE. I can see the future, okay? I can see the future and you totally will not make me feel good.

MAN IN THE DOWN COAT. Come on, Debbie. Don't be a [fucking tease.]

DEBBIE. [Whoa, who] the fuck is Debbie? Why does [everyone keep...?]

MAN IN THE DOWN COAT. [You just said,] you told me your name is Debbie.

DEBBIE. I probably lied. I can do that. I'm magic.

> *(She walks away. The* **MAN IN THE DOWN COAT** *lights a cigarette. He leans against the wall, clearly frustrated. Passing* **AARON** *and* **DAVEY**, **DEBBIE** *smiles at them and whispers confidentially. But her voice is amplified and has reverb.)*

There's blood falling from the sky. Shhhh.

> *(And then she's gone.)*

DAVEY. What the fuck?

AARON. It was just, it's the acoustics of the buildings [or the street.]

DAVEY. [The "acoustics] of the buildings?"

AARON. I don't know, I'm [trying to...]

DAVEY. [You don't have] to have an answer for [everything.]

AARON. [Look, can] we, can I just say this?

> *(He glances at the* **MAN IN THE DOWN COAT** *and steps closer to* **DAVEY**.*)*

So I'm not...emotive. Or I don't have access to, no that sounds bad, I just don't get super emotional. Or it doesn't come out. You know that. But it doesn't mean all of that isn't in here. You have to know that.

DAVEY. If it's only in there, how can you share it?

AARON. I don't know. I just don't want to be alone.

> *(Pause.)*

DAVEY. That's not... I think I'm gonna skip dinner.

AARON. Don't do that, it's gonna be okay.

DAVEY. We can't break up and then go to a fancy dinner. In Iceland. Even right now you've got your own version of me playing in your head.

> *(He steps into* **AARON** *and kisses him. It's a simple kiss goodbye. The* **MAN IN THE DOWN COAT** *sputters out a cough.)*

MAN IN THE DOWN COAT. Hey, ladies. Take it somewhere else.

AARON. What did he say?

DAVEY. Let's get out of here.

MAN IN THE DOWN COAT. That's it. Fly away, little faeries.

> *(***AARON*** *turns around and steps back towards the* **MAN IN THE DOWN COAT**. *He throws down his cigarette and stamps it out.)*

AARON. Can I help you with something?

DAVEY. It's fine, just, you don't know what he'll do.

MAN IN THE DOWN COAT. Listen to your little friend and keep moving.

DAVEY. We're leaving.

AARON. No. We were having a private moment.

MAN IN THE DOWN COAT. On a fuckin' public street.

DAVEY. Hey, it's not our fault you got turned down, okay? Just leave us alone.

MAN IN THE DOWN COAT. Fuck you. Fuck you. Take your sissy bullshit and get out of here before I kick your ass and your pussy boyfriend's ass for sport.

> *(***AARON*** *charges the* **MAN IN THE DOWN COAT** *and shoves him. The* **MAN IN THE DOWN COAT** *punches* **AARON** *in the stomach. He buckles. The* **MAN IN THE DOWN**

*COAT grabs his shoulder, but **AARON** knocks his hand away and punches him and he goes down. **AARON** then kicks the **MAN IN THE DOWN COAT** in the ribs. Hard.)*

AARON. Whose ass are you [going to kick?]

DAVEY. [Let's go, let's] go. Come on.

*(They start to leave when the **MAN IN THE DOWN COAT** coughs out…)*

MAN IN THE DOWN COAT. I'm gonna kill you. You fucking faggots.

*(As soon as the word is uttered, a piercing feedback noise fills the space and everything is bathed in red light. **AARON** spins around, kicks the **MAN IN THE DOWN COAT** repeatedly. He then falls on him and begins to beat him. It is merciless and primal. **DAVEY** watches from a safe distance, still and horrified.)*

*(As the piercing feedback noise and the red lights continue, a torrent of blood begins pouring from the space above the men, splashing all over the fight. It douses them as **AARON** pins the **MAN IN THE DOWN COAT**'s arms with his knees, uses both hands to force the **MAN IN THE DOWN COAT**'s mouth open, and then rips out one of his teeth. **AARON** screams.)*

*(As **AARON** falls back, tooth in hand and hyperventilating, the lights restore and the sound cuts out. They are both a bloody mess. The **MAN IN THE DOWN COAT** drags himself away, whimpering and broken.)*

(**AARON** *gets up and watches the* **MAN IN THE DOWN COAT** *crawl out of view. He then opens his hand and holds up the tooth. He turns and looks at* **DAVEY** *then crosses towards him.*)

(**DAVEY** *doesn't move but is clearly terrified.* **AARON** *is covered in blood and still breathing heavy as he offers* **DAVEY** *the tooth.*)

AARON. I don't know what to...

(**DAVEY** *carefully takes the tooth.*)

(*They look at each other.*)

(*They look at each other.*)

(**DAVEY** *passionately kisses* **AARON.**)

6.

Bittersweet (Part 2)

(SIGN READS: "A hidden room in the cellar of a nondescript building just off Hverfisgata.")

*(**HANK** is on the floor in the middle of the blood now onstage. Barefoot. His long underwear is open and his arm is pulled out of one side exposing a knife wound. It's still bleeding.)*

*(Two **AMBIANCE SISTERS** sit in chairs somehow outside of the space. The large tin can filled with knives is still between them. They are still reading and already humming their tune, the lights warm and alive.)*

(A bell rings three times in quick succession and then there is the sound of a lock opening.)

*(**ROBERT** enters. He is wet from the rain outside. He immediately rushes to **HANK**. This is followed by the sound of a lock closing.)*

ROBERT.   Oh my god! Hank! Are you okay? What happened in here? We have to get you some help. Did he just lock us in here? You [need a doctor!]

HANK. [I'm okay. I'm] okay.

ROBERT. You're not okay, you're [bleeding.]

HANK. [The last, the] last guys weren't very nice.

ROBERT. They attacked you?

HANK. You're wet. Is [it raining...?]

ROBERT. [Yes, yes, it's] raining outside, don't worry about [me. What happened?]

HANK. [There are some] bandages and stuff on a tray over on the bed. Can you just, can you help me bandage it up?

> (**ROBERT** *rushes over and finds a silver tray sitting on the bed with some bandages, cotton balls, and hydrogen peroxide. He brings the entire tray over, slipping in the blood. He bandages the wound.*)

ROBERT. There's so much blood.

HANK. They were bleeding, too.

ROBERT. What?!

HANK. I don't know! There were two guys, I started to do my thing, they seemed to be enjoying it. They seemed to be okay, only one of them spoke English. That one did all the talking, he just kept asking, "Are you feeling good?" It was a red flag; I'm so fucking stupid. Then all of the sudden, the other guy, the one who didn't talk, pulled out a knife. He started, he just started cutting the other guy and himself and then me.

> (**ROBERT** *finishes bandaging the wound.*)

ROBERT. This will do for now, but you need to see [a doctor.]

HANK. [I'll be okay.]

ROBERT. Hank, they could have killed you. I can't believe they just left you like this.

> (*He goes to the door and screams…*)

You can't just treat people like this! You need to get this kid to a doctor or I am going to tear [this place apart!]

HANK. [Robert, Robert,] please stop!

> (*Pause.* **ROBERT** *turns and looks at* **HANK**, *breathing heavy.*)

HANK. Help me to the bed? I'm kind of, I feel dizzy.

(*ROBERT helps **HANK** to the bed.*)

ROBERT. Just try to, I don't know, relax. Or be still.

HANK. I was... I was telling the truth the other day. Some of the things I said about being here. About...the people who run this place.

ROBERT. I thought that was just a game?

HANK. I didn't want to, there's a little truth in everything, you know? I've been thinking I have to get out of here, but it's so hard to trust anyone and I've been here for so long. I don't know how to not be here, does that make sense? But I also don't want to die when some client attacks me.

ROBERT. So you do want to leave?

HANK. It isn't going [to be easy.]

ROBERT. [Do you want] to leave?

HANK. Will you help me?

ROBERT. Anything you need.

HANK. Anything?

ROBERT. Yes.

(**HANK** *pulls **ROBERT**'s face in for a gentle kiss. It is a desperate intimacy.*)

HANK. So you'll...

(**HANK** *grins big. It's an "I told you so" kind of grin.*)

...rescue me?

(*Pause. **ROBERT** gets up and backs away from **HANK**. He looks at the blood on the floor, takes in the room, then back to **HANK**.*)

ROBERT. This isn't one of your fucking, is this all fake?

*(Suddenly the **AMBIANCE SISTERS** stop humming and the warm lights vanish, shifting back to the stark lighting from the last scene. **HANK** also releases his injury and drops all pretense of pain or fear. This is by far the most pleased with himself we've seen him.)*

HANK. I said you'd be back.

ROBERT. Is this, is this real blood?

HANK. When I saw your name I was determined to be ready for you. How was it? Did you feel excited and powerful? Did you [feel like a...?]

ROBERT. [That is a real] wound, I was just, that cut on your arm is real.

HANK. Sure. I cut myself.

(He pulls a small, bloody pair of shears from under his pillow.)

ROBERT. You cut yourself?

HANK. I mean, you can't fake getting stabbed if you [really want to sell...]

ROBERT. [You did this] to yourself?

HANK. You really need to get over that part, [Robert.]

ROBERT. [No, this is] too much blood for [you to have...]

HANK. [Oh sure, you'd be] amazed what they have sitting around here. Honestly, and I don't want you to feel vanilla or anything, but this isn't even the tip of the iceberg in terms of roleplay.

ROBERT. And the men you talked about?

HANK. I made them up. I mean, I've seen those kinds of men before, but none of that happened. Obviously.

ROBERT. You're insane.

(**HANK** *laughs.*)

You're insane!

HANK. You really bought it; I love that. I'm so good at making things up, making them real. Honestly, it makes me wonder if those men are actually out there in the world walking around now. I bet I could do that. What if I made them real? What if I invented two crazy men and [now they're...]

ROBERT. [Then you'd be] responsible for, fuck, why am I even engaging this bullshit? Why would you, why in the world would you think I'd like this?

HANK. Because you did.

ROBERT. I was terrified!

HANK. And you were ready to go full Prince Charming, whisk me away to safety, and then have sex. Tell me I'm wrong.

ROBERT. It wasn't like that.

HANK. Oh, okay.

ROBERT. I thought you were really hurt.

HANK. I'll tell you a secret, Robert. Nothing can hurt me here. You can't imagine what would happen if someone really tried to hurt me.

ROBERT. I wonder how many people have thought that exact same thing before dying some horrible death.

HANK. You're so melodramatic. I couldn't do what I do unless I had the confidence to know I'll be okay. So this place takes care of me.

ROBERT. This awful place?

HANK. Wait, awful?

ROBERT. It's fucking awful!

HANK. Awful?

ROBERT. Yes! The way you fuck with people, the depraved things that go [on in here when…]

HANK. [Depraved things that] left you exhausted and begging for more until a few minutes ago? Depraved things that you fucking loved and now you wanna call them awful? Well, this "awful" place is my home. This "awful" place takes care of me, so I don't need you to take care of me, Robert.

ROBERT. Fine.

> (**HANK** *smiles. It's not nice. He gets up and closes in on* **ROBERT.**)

HANK. I don't need you to do anything for me. I don't need you to help me, save me, rescue me. You can't do any of that, do you understand?

ROBERT. I said fine. Stop it.

HANK. No. I'm invincible here, I'm the god of this little room. And you are fucking nothing. Standing there judging this place, judging me, thinking you know more than me about how the world works. You have no idea what I've seen, how long I've, no, do you even know how old I am?

ROBERT. I know you're younger than me, I fucking [know you've…]

HANK. [Is that what you] think? Maybe I just look like this because it's exactly what you want? Maybe I'm completely different for every man that walks in that door. Because maybe I'm older than you could ever imagine, born from seawater splashing onto boiling hot lava rock, and that's why I can look at you and see how pathetic you are.

ROBERT. Fuck you.

HANK. No, fuck you. Fuck you for your moral condescension, fuck you for judging me when I just delivered your deepest desire, and fuck you for believing something secret and magical like me would ever choose such a lonely, broken, [desperate man!]

ROBERT. [Shut your mouth!]

> (**ROBERT** *smacks* **HANK** *across the face, hard, and then begins to choke him.* **HANK** *struggles, but* **ROBERT** *has come unhinged. He continues to strangle* **HANK** *as he walks him back to the bed.* **HANK** *chokes out...)*

HANK. Robert, if you don't stop [I won't be...]

ROBERT. [You think] you're powerful just because you're young and attractive and know how to use your dick? You think that makes you better than me?

HANK. Robert.

ROBERT. You think your neck won't fucking snap just like any other boy?

> (*Suddenly the* **AMBIANCE SISTERS** *get up. They each select a knife from the can between them, and then charge into the scene, causing the lights to flicker sporadically like the electricity is being interrupted.)*

> (*They grab* **ROBERT** *and pull him off* **HANK**. **HANK** *immediately curls up into a ball on the bed, covering his eyes. The* **AMBIANCE SISTERS** *drag* **ROBERT** *off into the darkness. His screams filter in from offstage. Eventually his screams stop. Pause.)*

> (**HANK** *uncovers his eyes and sits up on the bed. He catches his breath and calms. The* **AMBIANCE SISTERS** *come back in. Their hands and knives are bloody. They stop and look at* **HANK**. **HANK** *looks at them.)*

HANK. Is he...is he gone?

AMBIANCE SISTERS. My precious one, I took care of it for you.

HANK. He's dead?

AMBIANCE SISTERS. Soon. He's exsanguinating on the concrete in the storage room.

HANK. That's a shame.

AMBIANCE SISTERS. Even fantasies have consequences. He had all sorts of choices.

HANK. I shouldn't have pushed him like that. I was being cruel.

AMBIANCE SISTERS. Darling, cruelty is a part of your stock and trade.

HANK. But I liked...

(*The* **AMBIANCE SISTERS** *shoot* **HANK** *a look.*)

All right.

AMBIANCE SISTERS. You were being honest. And no one hurts my sweet boy.

HANK. Thank you.

AMBIANCE SISTERS. You are desire and beauty and you will never fade away.

HANK. Good.

AMBIANCE SISTERS. At least as long as people are willing to pay for it.

(**HANK** *smiles. Nervously.*)

HANK. You...you take such good care of me.

AMBIANCE SISTERS. Get yourself ready for the next customer. I'm going to go soak his body in lye for a little alkaline hydrolysis. The skin just falls off the bone.

AMBIANCE SISTERS. Then once he's melted away, I can pour him right into the ocean.

HANK. The ocean?

AMBIANCE SISTERS. Yes, love.

HANK. That's nice. I think he'd like that.

> *(The* **AMBIANCE SISTERS** *exit.* **HANK** *uses a handkerchief to wipe the blood off of the shears until they sparkle. He hums to himself. It's the same tune the* **AMBIANCE SISTERS** *were humming earlier.)*

7.

Wild Game

(SIGN READS: "A small bar in an alley just off Laugavegur a few minutes before four a.m.")

*(**GRIGOR** is softly singing into an large, vintage microphone on a stand. It's a very "lounge singer" vibe. It's clearly the end of the night. He has a cocktail in one hand and zones out while singing a torch song like "One Less Bell to Answer."[*] He seems much looser now. His hands are stained red with blood. **MARTIN** is near him, sipping a drink and looking on with adoration.)*

*(**INGRID** enters. She's in a black shirt and a black skirt. She has glasses and her hair is hanging in her face. She brings on a mop and starts to clean up the blood on the floor. After a moment, **INGRID** begins to quietly sing along with **GRIGOR** while mopping.)*

*(**VALERIE** enters in a similar outfit to **INGRID**, wearing flats, carrying a coat, a purse, and a pair of heavy, lace-up boots. She's on her way home. As soon as she appears, **INGRID** stops singing.)*

---

[*] A license to produce *Reykjavík* does not include a performance license for "One Less Bell to Answer." The publisher and author suggest that the licensee contact ASCAP or BMI to ascertain the music publisher and contact such music publisher to license or acquire permission for performance of the song. If a license or permission is unattainable for "One Less Bell to Answer," the licensee may not use the song in *Reykjavík* but should create an original composition in a similar style or use a similar song in the public domain. For further information, please see the Music and Third-Party Materials Use Note on page iii.

(**VALERIE** *stops short at the sight of the blood.*)

VALERIE. Oh wow. What's all this?

INGRID. Blood.

VALERIE. Blood?

INGRID. Bar fight right at closing. That's what I heard; I didn't see it. I got most of the glass, but be careful. Just in case.

VALERIE. Are you new?

INGRID. Yes.

VALERIE. Regretting taking the job yet?

INGRID. Oh, it's okay. I have a lot of jobs. I do sort of, I guess you'd call it a "tour guide" thing sometimes, I work in a hotel part time, and now this. Seems mostly fine so far.

VALERIE. Good. Good, hold on...

(*She turns to* **GRIGOR** *and shouts...*)

Hey! Give it a rest, call it a night.

MARTIN. Hey! Fuck you! We're not even real!

(**GRIGOR** *sits down with* **MARTIN.** *Maybe he sings quietly just to him, but the music keeps playing.*)

VALERIE. Great. They're in a mood.

INGRID. He has a nice voice.

VALERIE. I guess. So they gave the upbeat new girl the shit job of cleaning this up.

INGRID. I don't mind.

VALERIE. I'd quit.

(**INGRID** *laughs.*)

I haven't worked here long, so I should thank you for taking this one. Probably the only reason I'm not cleaning it up.

INGRID. It really doesn't bother me.

> (**VALERIE** *sits down, slips off her flats, puts them in her bag, and begins putting on and lacing up the boots.*)

VALERIE. Have we met before?

INGRID. I don't think so? You were pretty slammed all night.

VALERIE. I'm Valerie. Hey. I'm from the States.

INGRID. Ingrid. Nice to meet you.

> (*She holds out her hand.* **VALERIE** *shakes it.*)

VALERIE. Very formal.

> (**INGRID** *laughs.*)

When did you start?

INGRID. Oh, uh, I started a few nights ago now. It's been an adventure. I don't know if that's the right word. It's been a learning experience, especially anything that happens after three a.m.

VALERIE. Ah, the devil's hour.

INGRID. The what?

VALERIE. When bad luck sneaks in.

INGRID. I think it's just when people get really drunk.

VALERIE. That too. I'm sorry we haven't met yet; I've been in Edinburgh.

INGRID. Oh, I love Edinburgh.

VALERIE. Me too. Fun. I went back to settle a few kind of never-ending things with my ex-girlfriend. It's like, she thinks I'm gonna decide to move back.

INGRID. And you're not?

VALERIE. No way. I love it here. And I have this thing about only moving forward. In life, you know?

INGRID. No.

VALERIE. I move around a lot, it's hard to kind of stand still. But I only move to new places, no cheating and moving somewhere I've already been. There's too much world to experience.

INGRID. That's really pretty.

VALERIE. Yeah.

INGRID. But it sounds hard.

VALERIE. Does it?

INGRID. I don't know, just, it would be difficult for me. Letting go of things.

VALERIE. Oh, I get it. It's definitely not for everyone. But I guess I've never really been a "play it safe" kinda gal. Ugh, who the fuck even knows what that means? I'm a waitress in a bar. And now you already know everything about me, so you can tell what kind of over-sharer I am.

> (**INGRID** *laughs.* **VALERIE** *gets up, boots tied, ready to go. She collects her coat and purse.*)

INGRID. You've got...charisma.

VALERIE. Wow. Buy me a drink.

INGRID. What?

VALERIE. Oh no, I'm just saying that was nice, that was a flattering thing to say. So, like, "Hey, thanks. Buy me a drink." Never mind. Are you, are you sure we haven't met before?

INGRID. I'm really sure.

VALERIE. I'm having this super intense déjà vu, really intense.

INGRID. There are just people like me everywhere. I'm one of those people who just seems really familiar. People always think they already know me or recognize me, call me different names, you can't imagine. Or maybe there are just a lot of different "me"s running around in the world.

VALERIE. Huh. That sounds interesting.

INGRID. It's… Yes. I suppose it does sound interesting. Can I ask you something?

VALERIE. Shoot.

INGRID. I'm guessing these guys are regulars, but how long do they get to stay?

VALERIE. They'll probably call it a night when we turn the lights off. The door guy says they both have tempers so it's easier to just let them keep going.

INGRID. I don't mind the music, I actually enjoy it. But we're closed and he, um, he just keeps playing that same song over and over.

VALERIE. They started coming in recently, apparently. Just appeared out of nowhere while I was gone. Just like you. Who knows?

>	(**INGRID** *slow dances a bit with her mop and does a little turn.*)

INGRID. Let them have their fun, right?

VALERIE. That was lovely.

INGRID. Everyone says I'm very graceful with a bloody mop.

>	(*They both laugh.*)

VALERIE. I love your laugh.

INGRID. Do you?

VALERIE. Oh, I hope that's not too forward.

INGRID. I know you're not hitting on me.

> (**VALERIE** *pointedly sets down her coat and purse.*)

VALERIE. Do you?

INGRID. Oh.

VALERIE. You don't know me either, so how do you know?

> (**INGRID** *laughs again, this time more nervous.*)

INGRID. I'm dancing in blood.

VALERIE. It's unique.

INGRID. I hope so.

> (**VALERIE** *holds out her hand.*)

VALERIE. Ah, but what if we were both dancing in blood?

> (**INGRID** *cautiously takes it.* **VALERIE** *gives* **INGRID** *a twirl and the lights pulse up in the space for one magical turn.* **INGRID** *laughs.*)

And what if I was hitting on you?

INGRID. Well, then I suppose we'd have to go out. Get dinner or something...more conventional.

VALERIE. Where?

INGRID. Grillmarkaðurinn.

VALERIE. Expensive.

INGRID. That's right.

VALERIE. Luckily, I have a friend who manages there. And what are we eating?

INGRID. The wild game platter.

VALERIE. Hmm, I prefer the Minke whale. But I like game meat.

INGRID. Is that right?

VALERIE. I'll do duck or reindeer, but I don't eat goose. I don't want to chip my tooth on any pellet they don't find.

INGRID. You don't have to eat the goose.

VALERIE. Are you magic or something?

INGRID. Maybe I'm magic.

VALERIE. I like this date. I suppose I'm buying?

INGRID. Or we can split the check.

(**VALERIE** *steps even closer. Intimately close. She looks down at* **INGRID***'s necklace.*)

VALERIE. Wow, I used to have a necklace just like that one.

(**INGRID** *self-consciously handles the necklace.*)

INGRID. What a coincidence.

VALERIE. I got it from the first girl I ever dated. I lost it somewhere in...

INGRID. Yes?

(**INGRID** *steps back. Some of the lights shut out and the microphone cuts off with a pop.* **GRIGOR** *and* **MARTIN** *down their drinks and leave.* **VALERIE** *notices the changes, but* **INGRID** *doesn't look away from her. It's quiet now.*)

VALERIE. I'm... I do know you. I'm, okay, I'm not imagining this or whatever, where do I know you from?

INGRID. I don't know.

>   *(She pulls a band off her wrist, pulls her hair back, and puts it up.)*

VALERIE. Oh my god, you used to come into my bar in Edinburgh all the time.

>   (**INGRID** *takes off her glasses and pockets them.)*

INGRID. Did I?

VALERIE. Holy shit, you totally used to sit next to me at that coffee shop in Berlin every morning and read, what was it, oh what the fuck was it?

INGRID. *The Moral Animal.*

VALERIE. Yes!

INGRID. I've heard it's great, I should read it.

>   *(And suddenly **VALERIE** realizes...)*

VALERIE. What do you mean you, wait, wait, why didn't you say you knew me?

INGRID. I don't.

VALERIE. But you were in Edinburgh and Berlin.

INGRID. And Turin and Bern and Porto. You do move around a lot.

VALERIE. What?

INGRID. Why is that?

VALERIE. I always feel, no, it [sounds...]

INGRID. [Why is] [that?]

VALERIE. [You don't] [get to just...]

INGRID. [Why is that?]

VALERIE. I always feel like I'm being chased.

INGRID. Good. That was honest.

VALERIE. And I was right.

INGRID. But we don't know each other. Like I said, there are just people like me everywhere.

> *(Pause.)*

VALERIE. What do you want?

INGRID. I work here.

VALERIE. What do you want?

INGRID. I thought we were going to dinner?

VALERIE. Okay, cut the shit. You're following me all over the goddamn, what do you want?

INGRID. You.

> *(Pause.)*

It's not just me; it's all of us. The girls in Edinburgh, Berlin, Turin, Bern, Porto, all the girls exactly like me. The girls you didn't notice or passed by who could be the one.

> *(For just this one line, her voice is dubbed with a dozen different takes. All her, but not in unison. It's clear there are many voices. It's amplified and has some kind of reverb.)*

And we all want you.

> *(**VALERIE**'s breath catches in her chest and she takes a step back.)*

VALERIE. How did you do that?

INGRID. Do what?

VALERIE. With your voice, how did you...?

INGRID. That's just how I sound.

VALERIE. Okay. Okay, I should, I'm going to go.

INGRID. I'm confused. We were having a moment.

VALERIE. You've been stalking me!

INGRID. No, I haven't. I already explained [that to you.]

VALERIE. [No, no, you] didn't. No, you didn't.

INGRID. You seem to be thinking of this as threatening or like some kind of bad thing? It's really not. You called me lovely, didn't you?

VALERIE. Things change.

(*She starts to leave.*)

INGRID. Isn't this better than feeling chased?

(**VALERIE** *stops.* **INGRID** *presses on…*)

Leave if you want to leave, let me be another girl in another city you never knew. But if we have dinner and actually talk, that feeling might fade, that need to run you've convinced yourself is a choice.

(**VALERIE** *turns back.*)

Maybe you won't be afraid, maybe your heart won't race for no reason. Maybe I am magic and you won't need to run away anymore?

(*Pause.*)

VALERIE. Or I can move again.

INGRID. Or you can move again.

VALERIE. What about that?

INGRID. And again and again.

VALERIE. Fuck.

(**VALERIE** *turns back to* **INGRID**.)

The blood on the floor is like a bad omen or something.

INGRID. The devil's hour, right?

VALERIE. Was there...was there really a bar fight?

INGRID. Probably. But anyway, like you said...you've never really been a "play it safe" kinda gal.

VALERIE. I did say that.

INGRID. You've seen me so many times in so many places without seeing me. But tonight you did. You do. So this is it. Here I am. Here you are. And...?

(*Pause. As long as it takes.*)

VALERIE. I think... Oh god, okay, there's something about you that's, fuck. Okay. Okay, okay. I think... Fuck. I think that we can potentially go to dinner. Fuck. Tomorrow night. Maybe. Barring any other bizarre revelations.

INGRID. Really?

VALERIE. I don't know, no, it already feels crazy so I might change my mind.

INGRID. I'll make the reservation.

VALERIE. I'll make the reservation.

INGRID. Perfect.

VALERIE. Don't smile like you won or something; you didn't win anything.

INGRID. That's not why I'm smiling.

VALERIE. And if you do that thing with your voice again, I'm leaving.

INGRID. What thing?

VALERIE. The thing, the multitude of voices thing.

(**INGRID** *smiles.*)

INGRID. I don't know what you mean.

VALERIE. Ingrid.

INGRID. Deal.

(**INGRID** *holds out her hand to shake again.* **VALERIE** *can't believe she's doing this. She shakes* **INGRID***'s hand.*)

8.

Aurora Borealis

(*SIGN READS: "A rock outcropping with an exceptional view."*)

(**JAMES** *makes his way on. He's in a hoodie now with a heavier jacket over it. Nothing too bulky. He finds a place to sit then pulls his hood back. He's still sporting Debbie's pair of large faux gold headphones around his neck. He's been beaten. Badly. He takes a deep breath and then exhales, shaking out his arms.*)

(*After a moment, one of the* **HULDUFÓLK***, or Hidden People, enters and stands at distance behind him. A male, he is in a long gray trench coat, hands in pockets, with a black stripe painted across his eyes.*)

JAMES. I know you're back there.

HULDUFÓLK (M). But you can't see me. I'm hidden.

(**JAMES** *doesn't ever turn back to look at him.*)

JAMES. You're not as hidden as you think. Nice jacket, by the way.

HULDUFÓLK (M). Oh. I usually dress a bit more diaphanous, but this feels…"Western." And all of my people are hidden. But not to you. That is why I'm following you.

JAMES. Because I can see you?

HULDUFÓLK (M). In case I can be helpful.

JAMES. Huh, where were you last night?

HULDUFÓLK (M). Hidden.

JAMES. Great.

HULDUFÓLK (M). Inside of a large tea-leaved willow.

JAMES. Well, you're a little late to help.

HULDUFÓLK (M). I am sorry to hear that.

JAMES. Is this a good spot to see the northern lights?

HULDUFÓLK (M). It definitely can be. Is that why you're here?

JAMES. I'm finally gonna get this right.

HULDUFÓLK (M). The weather may not be your friend.

JAMES. Who are you?

HULDUFÓLK (M). Oh, I don't have a name.

JAMES. Perfect. Well, I'm James.

HULDUFÓLK (M). Hello, James. Have you heard of, ah, you would call them Adam and Eve?

JAMES. Everyone's heard of Adam and Eve.

HULDUFÓLK (M). Oh, that's nice to hear. Eve was the mother of my kind. And one day God came to see her children, but she didn't have time to clean all of us. The ones she couldn't make presentable for God, she hid. And because she hid us from God we remain hidden forever, moving through nature unseen.

JAMES. I'm not really religious.

HULDUFÓLK (M). Me either, as it happens.

JAMES. And I'm pretty sure I'm still fucked up.

HULDUFÓLK (M). The crisp air and natural beauty will sober you up.

JAMES. Everything's an advertisement for tourism. Fucking Iceland.

HULDUFÓLK (M). Anyway, it's still a good story.

JAMES. It's a sad story.

HULDUFÓLK (M). I suppose it is, but it's also what makes us special.

JAMES. Sure. I'd rather be happy.

>*(**NAOMI** enters. She is in a winter jacket with a hood up, covering her hair and hiding her face. She walks over and sits next to **JAMES**.)*

>*(They quietly sit next to each other. Her knee shakes. Anxious.)*

>*(After a moment, one of the **HULDUFÓLK** enters and stands at distance behind her. A female, she is in a long gray trench coat, hands in pockets, with a black stripe painted across her eyes.)*

>*(She looks over at her fellow **HIDDEN PERSON** and they nod.)*

I, uh... I didn't think anyone else would be up here.

NAOMI. It's pretty cold.

JAMES. Yeah.

NAOMI. But I'm always cold.

JAMES. Oh. I came to, uh, I'm trying to see the northern lights.

NAOMI. Because of the coffee table books?

JAMES. What?

NAOMI. What are you doing here?

JAMES. I told you, I'm here [to see...]

NAOMI. [James, what] are you doing here?

(**NAOMI** *pulls her hood back to reveal her thick braid and the hot pink stripe in her hair.* **JAMES** *is stunned to see his dead sister.*)

(*Pause. They stare at each other. She smiles. His eyes fill with tears. Her eyes fill with tears. This takes as long as it takes.*)

JAMES. Naomi?

NAOMI. Hey, little brother.

(*He hugs her. Tight.*)

JAMES. You're so cold.

NAOMI. You too.

JAMES. How is this, how are you...?

NAOMI. I'm here because you're here.

JAMES. I don't understand.

HULDUFÓLK (F). He doesn't know.

NAOMI. James, I just... I came to see the northern lights with you.

JAMES. We're finally here.

NAOMI. Yes.

JAMES. I wish I'd come sooner.

NAOMI. I'm glad you waited.

JAMES. This is gonna sound... Are you real?

NAOMI. Yes.

JAMES. Last night I was at this bar and some guys, I think they slipped something into my drink. Everything got hazy but we were...

NAOMI. Yes?

JAMES. We were having sex.

NAOMI. Okay.

JAMES. But I kept blacking out. I could feel these hands around my neck and I would black out and then come to again. But the hands were still there and they would squeeze and then I was gone again. It all feels like, I wanted to leave. I think I wanted to leave, but I couldn't move. So my head is all scattered and I'm not exactly trusting my, you know, I'm just not trusting all of this.

NAOMI. What happened after?

JAMES. I woke up near these rocks. I had planned to come here last night, was it last night? So I guess, I must have left the hotel and... I don't know.

(She covers her mouth.)

What is it?

HULDUFÓLK (F). He doesn't know.

NAOMI. Nothing.

JAMES. You look upset.

NAOMI. We have...we have plenty of time to piece it all together.

JAMES. You can stay with me?

NAOMI. You can stay with me.

JAMES. I can't stay in Iceland. I have to get home. My flight is later today. You should come with me.

HULDUFÓLK (F). You can't.

NAOMI. I can't.

JAMES. Why?

NAOMI. This is, just, I am real. Please don't get confused. And don't worry. We won't stay in Iceland.

JAMES. My head's still really, I don't think I understand.

NAOMI. Let's not talk about it.

JAMES. You're here now, I still can't... Can you tell me what happened to you?

NAOMI. Yes.

>   *(Pause.)*

JAMES. Will you?

>   (**NAOMI** *gets up and takes a few steps away.*)

You don't [have to...]

NAOMI. [No, it's] fine. You're fine.

>   *(She's trying to make it as painless to hear as possible. But it's hard to not get caught up in it again.)*

It was after midnight and I heard a knocking on that glass sliding door in my room. The one you would always let me back in through when I snuck out. I thought maybe the knocking was from one of the boys I was, I thought it might be someone I knew. But my bedroom lights were on, so outside the door was all darkness. That total blackness. Someone could have been standing inches from the door and I wouldn't have been able to see. So I turned on the exterior light and... nothing. I opened the door and there was nothing, just the wind and the snow. And the dark. But I definitely heard knocking. Then I saw the footprints. Or actually boot prints. They were leading away from my door into the woods behind our house. And they were new. Fresh. I took a few steps out of the door and I could feel the cold snow on my feet. I should have gone back inside, but instead I whispered into the night, "Is anyone...is anyone there?"

>   *(Pause.)*

JAMES. Naomi?

NAOMI. I heard a branch snap. Not a deer, it wasn't that soft sound a deer makes. Then suddenly a hand shot out of the darkness, a gloved hand. A man's hand. I didn't see his face, but he shoved his fingers into my mouth, gripped me by the jaw, pulled me a few feet, and slammed my face into a tree. And then nothing.

JAMES. Oh my god.

NAOMI. Oh no, it's okay.

JAMES. It's not okay.

NAOMI. James, there's nothing anyone can do about it now. You asked so I told you, but it didn't hurt. Or I don't remember it hurting. Okay? So focus on the good part. Here I am, with you right now. That's the good part.

JAMES. Since you disappeared I've been, when you disappeared, I looked for you every day after school, did you know? And I never found you.

NAOMI. That's not your fault.

JAMES. It absolutely is my fault. I let down Mom and Dad, I left school because I couldn't, because I didn't want to focus, I've done horrible things, I've let people do horrible things to me, I've let people do whatever they want and tell me that I'm pretty and special and none of it's true and I can't even find the fucking northern lights, the gigantic northern lights, because of clouds! I can't control the clouds and I can't do anything right!

> (**NAOMI** *hugs him tight, desperate to comfort him.*)

HULDUFÓLK (F). That's how you help.

HULDUFÓLK (M). That's how I help.

HULDUFÓLK (F). Not exactly conventional.

HULDUFÓLK (M). What is conventional?

>*(The* **HULDUFÓLK (M)** *waves his hand at the sky. The space is suddenly bathed by undulating green, blue and yellow light. It's the Aurora Borealis shining down. Dancing. All four of them look up.)*

JAMES. Oh wow.

NAOMI. It looks like the book.

JAMES. It's better than the book.

NAOMI. It is better than the book.

JAMES. I actually…I finished something. I did it. We did it.

>*(He smiles at her, looks up, and takes in the lights.)*

NAOMI. See? You don't fail at everything.

>*(She takes his hand and looks up at the lights with tears in her eyes.)*

But I wish you hadn't found me.

JAMES. They're just so…

HULDUFÓLK (M). [Beautiful.]

HULDUFÓLK (F). [Beautiful.]

End of Play